ARCHIE COMIC PUBLICATIONS, INC.

DEDICATED TO THE MEMORIES OF

MICHAEL I. SILBERKLEIT
CHAIRMAN/CEO/PUBLISHER
1932-2008

RICHARD H. GOLDWATER
PRESIDENT AND CO-PUBLISHER
1936-2007

VP/ EDITOR-IN-CHIEF
VICTOR GORELICK
VP/ DIRECTOR OF CIRCULATION
FRED MAUSSER
MANAGING EDITOR
MIKE PELLERITO
COMPILATION EDITOR
PAUL CASTIGLIA
ART DIRECTOR
JOE PEP

COVER ART
DAN DeCARLO
COVER COLORIST
ROSARIO "TITO" PEÑA
PRODUCTION
STEPHEN OSWALD
CARLOS ANTUNES
JOE MORCIGLIO

SIDE 1
STEREO
SOUND
FOR STEREO AND MONO
RECORD PLAYERS
33⅓
LP

THE Archies® "GREATEST HITS"

THE ARCHIES "GREATEST HITS" Volume 1, 2008.
Printed in Canada. Published by Archie Comic Publications, Inc., 325 Fayette Avenue, Mamaroneck, New York 10543-2318.

ISBN-13: 978-1-879794-37-5
ISBN-10: 1-879794-37-3

WWW.ARCHIECOMICS.COM

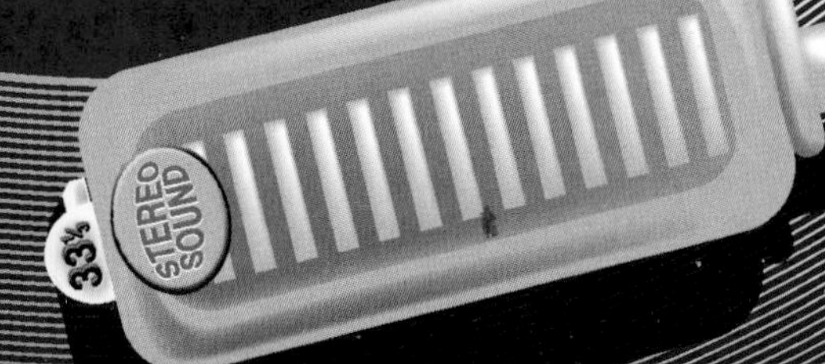

"EVERYTHING'S ARCHIE"

FOREWORD BY
RON DANTE

Archie's here, ba-ba-ba-ba-da, (that's the band playing). Betty's here, Veronica, too. Reggie's here, ba-ba-ba-ba-da, (that's the band again). Here comes Jughead and Hot Dog, too. So, everything's Archie!

That was the theme song I sang every Saturday morning on TV for three years. How did I end up as the lead singer of The Archies, you may ask? Well, it happened like this...

I grew up loving The Archies. I read their comic books all the way through grade school. Archie, Betty, Veronica, Reggie and Jughead were some of my best friends. They kept me company since I didn't have any brothers or sisters. They were like part of my family. Every Wednesday they arrived via their comic books at my favorite soda shop and I couldn't wait to read about all their many adventures in Riverdale.

Riverdale, that wondrous place where kids had fun playing in the park, going to the movies, congregating at the soda shop and where Archie hung out... hoping to meet girls. Riverdale, the town where kids cared about passing tests in school, worried about their grades, went to dances, had fun parties, and where Archie played on the football team... hoping to meet girls. Riverdale, it was where I lived in my imagination.

Every week I would run home carrying my Archie comics (which I still have today) and put them right beside my bed to read at night. There was something in those pages that made me feel happy. Each cover was an invitation to a magical place where I could escape for a while and live in a perfect world.

I read Archie comics all the way up to high school, until my taking tests and hoping to meet girls took precedence over reading about how Archie did it. He had taught me well. Archie and the gang had been my role models. They were everything I dreamed being a teenager would be like. Even though I had finally become a teenager myself with my own gang and set of friends, I never forgot my good pals in Riverdale and always carried a little bit of Archie with me everywhere I went.

combed my hair in a pompadour and never stopped looking for the right Betty or Veronica (didn't everyone?)

Music became my focus. Singing and writing songs helped me escape the hustle and bustle of everyday school life. All through my high school years I worked on my music.

I formed a group called The Detergents, which was the first pop group to sing parodies of then current hit songs. (before Weird Al did his) We went on tour with Dick Clark's Caravan of Stars in the mid 1960's. It was thrilling.

I eventually became a jingle singer singing on many famous commercials, some of which were, Dr. Pepper, McDonalds, Tang, American Airlines, Coca Cola, Pepsi and Campbell's Soup, just to name a few.

During that time, one of my musician friends told me that a company called Filmation was casting for a Saturday morning cartoon show and needed a lead singer.

I auditioned for music producers Don Kirshner and Jeff Barry, who were two of the most successful men in the music industry at that time. They loved my voice and felt I would be the perfect guy for the job. Low and behold, I was cast to be the lead singer of The Archies. (Some things are meant to be!) I felt like I was the luckiest singer in the world. I was to become the singing voice of my childhood hero, Archie. Talk about fate. I loved Archie and his friends. There I was, singing the Archies' theme song and all the hundreds of other songs to come for their TV show.

Each week on the show I would sing three songs: "Everything's Archie," the theme song of the show, a new hit song, and a song written for the dance of the week. Some of the dances were The Betty, The Veronica Walk, The Weatherbee, The Bubblegum, The Hamburger Hop and The Banana Split. There was also The Angel, The Rocketship and The Moonwalk. (long before Michael Jackson's)

The recording sessions we did for The Archies were some of most fun and exciting sessions I ever did. Along with the help of Ms. Toni Wine, the female voice of our group, The Archies were on their way.

Then came the hit song, "Sugar, Sugar." Wow! In 1969, "Sugar, Sugar" became the number one song worldwide, selling over six million copies, and was voted Billboard's number one record of the year. The Archies had arrived and I helped. (Could someone pinch me please?) The same week "Sugar, Sugar" went number one on the Billboard charts, Ed Sullivan, who hosted the most successful variety show on the air at that time, played the video of The Archies singing their hit song. The Archies were on top of the world and so was I.

Since then I have gone on to produce albums and songs for many top recording artists including Barry Manilow, Cher and Pat Benetar, but nothing has ever come close to my experience as the voice of The Archies.

The Archies' music was an entire generation's first exposure to pop music. Today, when I perform live and sing all the great songs of The Archies, fans of all ages come to me with smiles on their faces and tell me how important The Archies and their music have been to them over the years. Fans cannot seem to get enough of these great songs. It never ceases to amaze me, that even today I experience how happy fans become remembering their favorite band, talking about their comic books and rocking out to their favorite songs.

I'd like to thank everyone at Archie Comics for inviting me to write the foreword for "The Archies Greatest Hits". It has been such a joy to remember just how much Archie and his gang from Riverdale have meant to me.

No matter what I have accomplished in my career as a producer, a songwriter and a singer, nothing has ever delighted me as much as being the singing voice of Archie Andrews.

Archie, Betty, Veronica, Reggie, Jughead and the rest of the gang will always be my closest friends.

Here's to that special place, Riverdale. May it live on forever.

THE Archies in Music SOOTHES
BAYBEH, KISS ME HARD 'N' FAST, HOL' ME TIGHT AN' MAKE IT LAST, LOVE IS ALL AN' ALL IS LOVE, IT TURNS A HAWK INTO A DOVE
IT'S NOT THAT I DON'T LOVE THESE OLD CLASSICS, BUT MY TEETH ARE BEGINNING TO RATTLE!
AND I JUST PUT A CAKE IN THE OVEN!
1

THIS IS SNEAKY, BUT IT'S BETTER THAN HURTING THEIR FEELINGS!
FUSE BOX

HEY! THE AMPS HAVE GONE DEAD!
WE HAVE NO JUICE!
The Archies

BLOWN FUSE, BOYS! ...AND I DON'T HAVE A SPARE!
I'LL BE BACK WITH A NEW ONE IN AN HOUR OR SO!

AN HOUR WILL COOL THE CREATIVE SPARK!
OH?
SORRY, POP! ...WE CAN'T WAIT!

A FINE GROUP OF BOYS! ...AND EXCELLENT MUSICIANS! .... I THINK!
WHY DO THEY ALWAYS PLAY, ..."MUSIC TO BREAK EARDRUMS BY?"
2

HALT! I APPRECIATE MUSIC AS MUCH AS THE NEXT MAN!
POP'S CHOCKLIT SHOP

...BUT THAT STUFF YOU GAVE OUT LAST TIME CURDLED MY CREAM!

WE'RE LIVING IN A CULTURAL DESERT!
ALL CREATIVITY STIFLED BY THE ESTAB-LISHMENT!
YOU'RE MOVING ME TO TEARS!

BUT YOU'RE NOT MOVING INSIDE MY SHOP WITH THOSE NOISEMAKERS!
HEY! WHY DON'T WE PLAY OUT HERE?

ARE YOU NUTS? WHO CAN MAKE MUSIC WITHOUT ELECTRICITY?
I FORGOT!
NO PROBLEM!

I HAVE A LONG EXTENSION CORD!
YOU MEAN WE CAN PLUG IN ON YOUR JUICE?
3

YOU'RE ALL HEART, POPS!
THAT'S KIND OF YOU, ARCHIE! ACTUALLY, THOUGH, I'M ALMOST ALL FLAB!

OKAY! NOW HIT IT! A-ONE, A-TWO...
The Archies

WHAT A LOVELY FEELING!...TO BE ABLE TO TURN DOWN THE VOLUME JUST BY CLOSING THE DOOR!
OOOH! IT'S THE STREET WHERE WE MEET AND LAY ON THAT BEAT.. IT'S THE SIDEWALK SERENA-ADE

WHIRR!
WHAT THE...?

ZOOM!
4

THANKS, POPS!...BUT THIS IS TOO DANGEROUS!
POP'S
CHOCKLIT
SHOP

WHY DON'T YOU PRACTICE AT MY HOUSE?
BETTY!...YOU ARE A TRUE PATRON OF THE ARTS!

ISN'T IT GROOVY, MOM? THE ARCHIES ARE GOING TO PLAY RIGHT HERE! ...IN OUR HOUSE!
URK!

IT'S, LIKE, TOO MUCH! EEEE! I CAN BARELY STAND IT!
FUNNY! ALMOST THE VERY WORDS I WOULD HAVE USED!

POPPER DOPPER TEENY BOPPER EENY MEENY MINEY MO! PHONEY BONEY, MACARONI. GO, MAN, GO!
EEP!
5

ER... ARCHIE!... THERE'S JUST NO MEETING OF THE MINDS WITH THE OLDER GENERATION!
I'M AFRAID MOM'S ABOUT TO LOWER THE BOOM!

HAVING LOVE IN OUR HEARTS DOESN'T MEAN NO SMARTS IN OUR HEADS, BETS!
LEAVE THIS TO THE ARCHIES!

OH, SHE'S KINDLY AND GENTLE, SHE'S JUST SUPER DUPER!... IF YOU HAD HER YOU'D WANT FOR NO OTHER! THE BEST OF THE BEST IS OUR OWN, MRS. COOPER, THE EXQUISITE MODEL OF MOTHER!
The Archies

WHAT? I CAN'T HEAR YOU ABOVE THAT DIN!
I SAID, AREN'T THEY GROOVY? ...JUST TOO MUCH! I COULD LISTEN TO THEM ALL NIGHT!
THE END
6

THE Archies IN GROUP GRIPE

I CAN'T BELIEVE IT! THE ARCHIES HAVEN'T REHEARSED IN MONTHS!
THEIR DEAFENING DIN USED TO DROWN US OUT!
WE COULDN'T REHEARSE PROPERLY!
Schubert TRIO

SINCE WE'VE HAD THIS QUIET, OUR TRIO HAS MADE *TREMENDOUS PROGRESS!*

I DO BELIEVE WE'RE READY FOR A CONCERT!
YES, BUT WE'LL NEED MONEY FOR PROMOTION AND TO HIRE A HALL!

I'M ONE STEP AHEAD OF BOTH OF YOU! I CLEARED OUT MY ATTIC!
HOW IS THAT GOING TO GET MONEY FOR OUR CONCERT?

OBSERVE!
WEATHERBEE'S GARAGE SALE
2

I HATE TO DISILLUSION THE OLD BOY, BUT HE WON'T RAISE ENOUGH MONEY TO LIGHT THE SIGN OVER THE CONCERT HALL TICKET WINDOW!
WHO WOULD WANT THIS OLD JUNK OF HIS?
WEATHERBEE'S GARAGE SALE

ARCHIE, WHY DON'T I HEAR YOU REHEARSE ANYMORE?
WE'VE GOTTEN STALE, SIR!

IF WE DON'T FIND A NEW IMAGE, THE ARCHIES ARE FINISHED!
WONDERFUL!

ER---I MEAN--- WHILE YOU'RE SEARCHING FOR THIS "NEW IMAGE," WHY NOT LOOK OVER MY GARAGE SALE?
WHY NOT?
EATHERBEE'S GARAGE SALE

HEY, GUYS! DIG THESE FUNKY TAILS FROM THE THIRTIES!
VRA
WE DO OUR PART
MEMBER
U.S.
3

AND STILL IN AS GOOD SHAPE AS EVER, I MIGHT ADD!

IF I COULD SAY THE SAME, I'D STILL BE WEARING IT!

WOZ
DIG ALL THESE BITS OF NOSTALGIA!
AND THESE FAR-OUT CLOTHES!

GAD! THOSE KIDS BOUGHT OUT WEATHERBEE'S ENTIRE STOCK!
WHICH SAYS MUCH ABOUT THE GULLIBILITY OF TODAY'S YOUTH!

THERE'S ONE THING YOU CAN SAY ABOUT TODAY'S YOUTH!
---THEY RECOGNIZE QUALITY!
4

WE NOW HAVE ENOUGH MONEY TO GO AHEAD WITH OUR CONCERT PLANS!
I'LL BE DARNED!

ALL WE NEED IS ANOTHER MONTH OF GOOD, SOLID REHEARSING!

GOOD HEAVENS! WHAT WAS THAT?

IT SOUNDS LIKE THE ARCHIES HAVE STARTED UP AGAIN!
BUT I THOUGHT THEY WERE THROUGH!

WE *WERE* THROUGH UNTIL THAT GARAGE SALE OF YOURS!
YOUR FUNKY DUDS GAVE US THE *NEW IMAGE* WE WERE SEARCHING FOR!
The Archies
VRA
MEMBER
U.S.
THE END

THE Archies
VISIT TO A SMALL PANIC
FILMATION
HEY! THAT'S IT! LOOK! THAT'S WHERE THEY MAKE OUR T.V. SERIES..."THE ARCHIES"!
IF ONLY DADDY HADN'T SHIPPED THIS RUSTY OLD RATTLE-TRAP OUT HERE WITH US!
PUBLICITY, GIRL! GOT TO RETAIN THE ARCHIES IMAGE!
OOOH! FEEL THAT CALIFORNIA SUNSHINE!

NORM!... LOU!... I WANT OUT OF THE ARCHIE SERIES!
WHAT'S WRONG, HAL?

I'VE DIRECTED PURPLE DUCKS AND LUMPY CAMELS, SEXY SNAKES AND MANGY MONGOOSES.. ER MONGEESE ...UH...WHATEVER...

...BUT NONE OF THEM EVER BEFORE WADDLED, AMBLED, OR SLITHERED UP NORTH HOLLYWOOD AND STARED AT ME FROM DOWN ON THE STREET!
?

NORM!... LOU! THEY'VE COME TO LIFE!
SOMEBODY'S SCREAMING UP THERE!

HAL! GET HOLD OF YOURSELF! THE ARCHIES ARE FOR REAL!
YOU'RE PUTTING ME ON!
2

MR. LODGE FLEW THEM OUT FOR A TOUR OF THE STUDIO TO SEE HOW WE DO THE ARCHIE SHOW ON TV!
YOU MEAN "THE ARCHIES" REALLY EXIST? LOU WASN'T PUTTING ME ON?

WE-L-L, THEY PROBABLY AREN'T AS KOOKY AS WE MAKE THEM IN THE CARTOON SERIES!
LET'S GET THEM UP HERE AND FIND OUT!

THEY'RE PROBABLY WELL BEHAVED, MILD MANNERED YOUNGSTERS!
GOOD MUSICIANS, TOO!
SENSITIVE ARTISTS!

CRASH!

... BUT TERRIBLE DRIVERS!
YOU LEANED RIGHT IN FRONT OF ME! I COULDN'T SEE!
I THOUGHT I SAW A MOVIE STAR!
3

I'M HAL SOUTHERLAND, THE DIRECTOR OF YOUR SHOW, AND THIS IS LOU SCHEIMER AND NORM PRESCOTT, THE PRODUCERS!
HI!
GROOVY PLACE!
WHERE'S THE GUY WHO DRAWS ME? I WANT HIM TO USE MORE OF MY CLASSIC PROFILE!

GOLLY! YOU GENTLEMEN SURE KNOW YOUR BUSINESS! THE T.V. SHOW'S A SMASH!
BEST THING THAT EVER HIT SATURDAY MORNING!
THANK YOU, GIRLS!
EMERGENCY EXIT

NOW IF YOU'LL FOLLOW US WE'LL SHOW YOU HOW WE PUT THE SHOW TOGETHER!
?

EDITORIAL
AREN'T THEY A HOWL? THIS IS THE FUNNIEST ANIMATED CARTOON I EVER WORKED ON!
(GIGGLE!) THOSE ARCHIES ARE A WILD BUNCH OF CHARACTERS!
4

HI THERE, CHICKS!
HELLOOH!
WHERE'S THE CAFETERIA?

AIEEEEE! THEY'VE COME TO LIFE!
JUMPY LITTLE THINGS, AREN'T THEY?

GAK! WHAT HAPPENED HERE?
I PRESSED A BUTTON! I THOUGHT I'D GET A GLASS OF ROOT BEER!

MR. PRESCOTT!... MR. SCHEIMER! HELP! COLLECT THIS NUT! HE THINKS HE'S A LIVE REGGIE MANTLE!

WE'VE BEEN WORKING TOO HARD, CHARLIE! I'M BEGINNING TO SEE THESE CHARACTERS EVERYWHERE!
ME, TOO! I'M TAKING A VACATION!

THEY'RE DISRUPTING THE WHOLE PLACE!
WE'LL NEVER MEET OUR DEADLINES!
SOMETHING'S GOT TO BE DONE!
5

BOYS, OUR TOUR GUIDES ARE GOING TO SHOW YOU AROUND HOLLYWOOD!
THERE AIN'T NO-PLACE I WOULDN'T FOLLOW A GUIDE LIKE THAT!

NOW JUST A DOGGONE MINUTE!
OH, WE HAVEN'T FORGOTTEN YOU GIRLS!

THESE BOYS WILL SHOW YOU AND BETTY THE SIGHTS THAT PARTICULARLY APPEAL TO WOMEN!
GULP! OH, THEY CERTAINLY DO!

FOR YOU, JUGHEAD,... A CREDIT CARD TO ALL THE BEST HOLLYWOOD RESTAU-RANTS!... WITH A CAR AND CHAUFFEUR TO DRIVE YOU THERE!
LEAVE US NOT TARRY!

WHEW! NOW MAYBE WE CAN GET BACK TO NORMAL! WHAT A KOOKY CREW!
THEY'RE EVEN CRAZIER THAN WE MAKE THEM ON T.V.! ...AND WE WERE WORRIED ABOUT EXAGGERATING!
WE'D BETTER GO RIGHT ON EXAGGERATING! NOBODY WOULD EVER BELIEVE THE TRUTH!
The End

THE Archies -in- MISTER APPETITE
OKAY, TRIBE! LET'S RUN THROUGH NUMBERS SIX, SEVENTEEN, AND TWENTY! WE'RE A LITTLE WEAK ON THOSE!
SPEAK FOR YOURSELF, MIGHTY LEADER!... MANTLE IS EXCELLENT AT EVERYTHING!
The Archies

FLOOMPH!

FOOD!... IN MY GUITAR! JUGHEAD! YOU'VE BEEN STASHING YOUR GOODIES IN MY MUSIC MAKER AGAIN!

OH, THAT JUGGIE! ALWAYS SQUIRRELING THINGS AWAY!
REG!... JUG!... COME BACK! WE'VE GOT TO PRACTICE FOR TONIGHT'S DANCE!
IF I CATCH YOU YOU'LL HAVE FRUIT SALAD COMING OUT OF YOUR EARS!
DON'T BRUISE THE PEACHES!

HOW CAN HE RUN SO FAST WITH ALL THE FOOD HE PACKS AWAY?

WHAM!

ANYBODY EVER TELL YOU IT'S IMPOLITE TO EAT AND RUN?... ESPECIALLY IN MY HALLS!

IT WAS JUGHEAD'S FAULT, SIR!... BLAME HIM!
REALLY?
2

WE ARCHIES WERE ALL SET FOR A NICE PRACTICE SESSION AND OL' TROUBLE-MAKER JUG STARTS...
YOU MEAN YOUR DRUMMER?
BIPPITY! BOOM! BOOM!
The Archies

HUH? B-BUT HE WAS JUST TEARING THROUGH THE HALLS AND...
HMMM!
TZING!

WHY DON'T YOU STOP TRYING TO GET INNOCENT PEOPLE INTO TROUBLE?
...AND YOU'RE HOLDING UP PRACTICE!
GRRRR!

FINE!...NOW ISN'T THAT MORE FUN THAN MAKING TROUBLE FOR YOUR FRIENDS?

OH, I'M GONNA GET YOU! OH-H-H HOW I'M GONNA GET EVEN!
3

WHAT THE ?... I THOUGHT I GOT ALL THAT FRUIT OUT!
RATTLE! RATTLE!

OOPS!... ONE MISERABLE GRAPE, I MISSED!

PLOK!
PING!

YOU JUST DON'T KNOW WHEN TO QUIT, DO YOU, REGGIE?
MR. WEATHERBEE! IT'S NOT MY FAULT!

IT'S THAT JUGHEAD! HE PUT THE FOOD IN MY GUITAR!
NOW I KNOW THAT'S NONSENSE!

JUGHEAD NEVER PUTS FOOD INTO ANYTHING BUT JUGHEAD!
4

YOU'RE COMING TO THE END OF YOUR ROPE, BOY!... WATCH IT!

GRRR!... JUGHEAD AND HIS BOTTOMLESS STOMACH! HE'LL TURN THE WHOLE PLANET INTO A GARBAGE D...

..UMP!
ZWIP!

MY BANANA!... YOU RUINED MY BANANA!

NO! NO! BREAK IT UP!
TAKE FIVE! COOL IT!

I'LL TAKE A WALK TO COOL OFF! I THINK I'LL GO TO THE CAFETERIA AND GRAB A SMALL SNACK!
BRING ME SOME NICE, RICH, GOOEY DESERT, DARLING!
5

I DON'T KNOW HOW I CAN EVEN LOOK AT FOOD AFTER ALL THE TROUBLE IT CAUSED ME TODAY!
CAFETERIA

BUMP!

ALL OF YOUR LITTLE JESTS TODAY SEEM TO HAVE FOOD AS THEIR CENTRAL THEME!
YOU'RE TRYING TO BUG POOR JUGHEAD, AREN'T YOU?

ONE MORE LITTLE FOOD GAG, BOY, AND YOU'VE HAD IT!... NOW LAY OFF JUGHEAD AND GET ON WITH YOUR PRACTICING!
IS THAT SMOKE COMING OUT OF HIS EARS?
I DO BELIEVE HE'S OVERWROUGHT!
TZING! TZING! TZING!
The Archies
THE END

THE Archies in "The Last Chord.."

MAYBE NO GOOD! BUT I'VE GOT TO DO IT!
IT'S LIKE A HUNGER STRIKE!

PLEASE, ARCH! I GET WEAK WHEN SOMEONE MENTIONS CRUEL TORTURES LIKE THAT!

IT DOESN'T COUNT UNLESS YOU GIVE UP SOMETHING YOU LOVE AND NEED! LIKE MY MUSIC!

...OR JUGHEAD GIVING UP FOOD!
ARCH! DON'T!

HEY! IT GOT AWAY FROM US!
OOPS!
I HATE TO SAY IT TO MY BEST BUDDY, BUT IT SERVES HIM RIGHT!
WHOCK
ZOOM!
2

YOU GAVE UP YOUR GUITAR, BUT YOUR GUITAR DIDN'T GIVE UP YOU!
HYUK!
GROAN!

LOOK AT THAT! IS THAT ANY PLACE FOR PEOPLE TO LIVE?
IT IS PRETTY AWFUL!

NOW THAT'S A PLAYGROUND FOR THOSE KIDS! HOW DOES THAT GRAB YOU?
IT MAKES ME SICK!

I AGREE WITH YOU THAT THERE IS TOO MUCH MISERY IN THE WORLD!

BUT I DON'T SEE HOW DISBANDING THE ARCHIES IS GOING TO CURE IT!
I DIDN'T SAY IT WOULD CURE IT!
3

BUT IF THOSE KIDS CAN'T BE HAPPY, THEN I'M NOT GOING TO BE HAPPY EITHER!
BIG DEAL! HE'S GOING TO MAKE MORE MISERY!

AW NUTS!
EATS

LOOK! I'LL BET HE FOUND THAT OLD WRECK OF A GUITAR ON SOME GARBAGE HEAP!
ALL RIGHT! LET'S CUT OUT THE SOAP OPERA!

HUH?
THAT KID DOESN'T WANT SYMPATHY! HE WANTS HELP!
YOU'RE THE GUITAR MAN!

YOU'RE RIGHT, FOR PETE'S SAKE!
LET ME SEE THAT, KID!

HMMM! STRINGS ARE WHOLE, BUT LOOSE! THE NECK ISN'T IN THE BEST OF SHAPE!
CAN YOU FIX IT, MISTER?
4

I THINK THIS CORD MIGHT TIGHTEN THAT NECK TEMPORARILY!

NOW IF WE CAN JUST GET IN TUNE...
PLINK
PLUNK

NOT BAD! NOT BAD AT ALL!
HEY, CHARLIE! THIS GUY IS GOOD!

HEY, THAT'S COOL, MAN! KEEP IT GOIN!!
SAM! C'MERE!

JUGGIE! HE'S BUILDING AN AUDIENCE!
I DIG, BETTY! I DIG!
5

OH, THIS IS THE KIND OF SESSION THAT REALLY TURNS THE ARCHIES ON!
JUST PICK UP ON HIS BEAT!

?

HOW DID THEY ALL GET HERE?
HAD TO SHOW YOU THE ERROR OF YOUR WAYS, DINGALING!
YOU WANTED TO JOIN THEM IN THEIR MISERY!

...INSTEAD OF LETTING THEM JOIN YOU IN YOUR HAPPINESS!
HEY! IT DOES MAKE MORE SENSE, DOESN'T IT?
MAN! THAT'S GROOVY!
LET IT ALL HANG OUT!
THE ARCHIES IS WHERE IT'S AT!
The Archies
The END

THE Archies IN "LABOR of LOVE"

ALL RIGHT! COOL IT, BOYS! PUT A LID ON IT!

CAN'T YOU SEE I'VE GOT A CUSTOMER? EVERYBODY DOESN'T DIG THAT RACKET!

I DO! IN FACT, I'D LIKE TO HIRE THEM!
YOU WANT TO BREAK A LEASE?

I MANAGE THE ROVING EYE DISCOTHEQUE!
BINGO!

BETTY! VERONICA! DID YOU HEAR THAT? WE'VE GOT A BOOKING!
WONDERFUL, ARCHIEKINS! WE'LL HAVE SO MUCH FUN, SPENDING YOUR SALARY!!
YOU CAN START TONIGHT! I'LL BOUNCE THOSE SOUNDLESS SLOBS I'VE GOT NOW!
1.95
2

MAN! WE'RE REALLY PACKING THEM IN!
THERE'S NO BIZ LIKE SHOW BIZ!
THE ROVING EYE

HEY! IT'S THE ARCHIES!
PLUG IN AND GIVE OUT, GUYS!

YOU'D BETTER BE GOOD! WE HAD TO PAY TO HEAR YOU TONIGHT!

OH, BILLIE JO, I LOVED YA SO, I FELT SO MUCH ALIVE, SO TELL ME WHY YA HAD TO GO AN' TAKE THAT AWFUL DIVE?
3

HEY! HEY, ARCH! SMARTEN UP! YOU MISSED YOUR CUE!

HYUK! THE OL' REDHEAD IS TURNING PURPLE WATCHING RONNIE AND THE BOSS!

HOW LONG HAVE YOU HAD THAT BEE TATTOOED ON YOUR FACE?
IT'S A DECAL, LONG-SNOOT! IT'S THE LATEST THING!

SEE? BETTY'S GOT ONE, TOO!
WHAT'S THE WORLD COMING TO?

WHY DOESN'T THAT JOKER LEAVE MY GIRL ALONE AND GO TEND TO BUSINESS?
STICK TO YOUR STRUMMIN,' SUCKER! THAT'S WHAT'S BRINGING IN THE BREAD!
4

ARCH! WHAT ARE YOU DOING?
DON'T BOTHER ME!

TWANG!
OUCH!
WAP

I'VE BEEN STUNG! IT FELT LIKE A BEE, OR...

...THERE IT IS!
SLAP!
BOOM!
5

MAN! RIGHT ON THE TATTOO!
WE'D BETTER TAKE FIVE!!

YOU BOYS SOUND GREAT!
I DIDN'T THINK YOU WERE LISTENING!

HEY! LOOK!
IT'S THE CASHIER!
GET THAT GAG OUT OF HER MOUTH!
MMMPH!..SNKLFT.. BRRRTZZ!!!

ROBBED! WE'VE BEEN ROBBED! A MASKED HOOD STOLE ALL THE MONEY!!

HOW MUCH DID HE GET?
AT LEAST EIGHT HUNDRED DOLLARS!
WHAT'D HE LOOK LIKE?
6

MAN, HE WAS WEARING THE CRAZIEST SET OF THREADS!
LIKE WHAT?

INDESCRIBABLE!
WAIT! I'LL DRAW A PICTURE!

THERE! ISN'T THAT THE WILDEST OUTFIT?

HMPH! SOME KIND OF EXHIBITIONIST!

HE OUGHTTA BE EASY TO CATCH!
SURE! HE'LL STICK OUT LIKE A SORE THUMB IN THAT RIG!
7

HE ALSO HAD AN ARROW TATTOO ON HIS WRIST!
WHAT GOOD IS THAT?
FL

THOSE TATTOOS ARE DECALS! THEY CAN BE REMOVED!
REGGIE'S RIGHT!

HEY!
PART OF THE EIGHT HUNDRED WAS OUR PAY!

T-U-F, BOYS! THAT'S HOW THE OL' BALL BOUNCES!

THIS OUTFIT'S BEEN MAKING A MINT! YOU CAN STILL AFFORD TO PAY US!
YEAH! WE DEMAND OUR SALARY!
OUT! CRUMBS! WE'RE CLOSING UP FOR THE NIGHT!
8

MAN! I'D LIKE TO GET MY HANDS ON THE CROOK WHO STOLE OUR DOUGH!
ALL THAT WORK FOR NOTHING!
THE ROVING EYE

WOULD YOU LIKE TO KNOW WHO HAS ALL YOUR MONEY?
YOU KNOW?

THAT MANAGER FLASHED A TATTOO OF AN ARROW ON HIS WRIST WHILE WE WERE DANCING! A REAL ONE!

WHY, THAT CREEP! HE'S ROBBING THE OWNER OF THE DISCO!
DISGUISED IN THAT SQUARE JOHN OUTFIT, NOBODY KNEW HIM!

HE'LL BE TAKING THE MONEY HOME WITH HIM! WHAT SAY WE WAIT?
WHO'S GOING?

HYUK! NOT BAD FOR A NIGHT'S WORK! AN EIGHT HUNDRED DOLLAR BONUS!
9

AND THE STUPID OWNER IS INSURED, SO IT'S NO LOSS TO HIM!

THE BEAUTY PART IS, NOBODY EVER SUSPECTS THE MANAGER OF KNOCKIN' OVER HIS OWN JOINT!

WHOOPS
ER - WHAT THAT IS THERE, MISTER, IS GREASE IN WHICH YOU'RE SLIPPIN'!

THE GREASE! IT CAME FROM THE BUCKET IN WHICH YOUR FOOT IS NOW JAMMED!
SPLOOSH!

YOU!...YOU GREASED THAT STEP, YOU...

EEYURK!!
SPLAT
WHOOSH!

MY! MY! DO LOOK AT ALL THAT MONEY! I DO BELIEVE THIS BEARS INVESTIGATING!
SOB

AS OWNER OF THE ROVING EYE, I OWE YOU BOYS A DEBT OF GRATITUDE! NAME YOUR OWN REWARD!

OH, WE'RE NOT RICH, BUT WE'RE NOT GREEDY, AND WE MAY LOOK A TRIFLE SEEDY! BUT LET US PLAY AND WE'RE NOT NEEDY, FOR THIS IS LIVIN', YES INDEEDY!
AMAZING! THE ONLY REWARD THEY WANTED WAS A CHANCE TO WORK!
THERE'S A LOT MORE TO THE ARCHIES THAN MEETS THE EYE, MISTER!
The ARCHIES
THE END

THE Archies in "DRUM ROLL"

HEY! LOOKIT!
DRUMS!

HEY - HEE HEE - WE'RE ON A NEAT HILL! BETCHA THEY'D ROLL REAL GOOD!
LET'S SEE!

ACK! YOU CRAZY KIDS! THOSE THINGS COST A FORTUNE!!
ZOOOM

I HOPE THEY LAND IN A NICE SOFT HEDGE!

OH, NO!!
CRASH
2

THE ARCHIES ARE WITHOUT A DRUMMER!
HE COULD BEAT OUT THE RHYTHM BY THUMPING ON HIS HEAD!
HYOK!
The Archies

WE CAN'T AFFORD A NEW SET OF DRUMS! THE WORK ON THE VAN TOOK THE LAST OF OUR BREAD!

AND ---
WHAT'D YOU COME FOR? YOU GOT NOTHING TO DO!
SHUCKS! I'M STILL PART OF THE ARCHIES!

YOUR VOICE ISN'T TOO HORRIBLE, JUGGIE! HOW ABOUT SINGING THE NEXT NUMBER?
YOU THINK---?

OH, FINE! THAT'LL BE THE KISS OF DEATH FOR THE ARCHIES!
YOU NEVER KNOW WHAT'S GONNA TURN THE PUBLIC ON!

SOME OF THE MOST SUCCESSFUL SINGERS AROUND TODAY HAVE VOICES YOU COULD FILE YOUR NAILS WITH!
3

HEY! LISTEN TO THAT SOUND!
I DIDN'T KNOW THE ARCHIES HAD A SINGER!

THAT DEEP, THROATY SOUND!
LIKE TIRES ON A GRAVEL DRIVEWAY!
SEXY!

OH, WOW!
ISN'T HE MARVELOUS?
SING IT, BABY, SING IT!

HERE HE COMES NOW!
JUGHEAD!
I WANT HIS AUTOGRAPH!

HEY! LAY OFF!!!
SORRY, LOVER! I'VE GOT TO HAVE A SOUVENIR!
I GOT HIS HAT!
HE EVEN YELLS SEXY!
4

YOU'RE A SENSATION, JUGGIE!
THEY RIPPED MY CLOTHES!

IT'S NICE TO BE FAMOUS, BUT ALL THOSE GIRLS! UGH!

I'LL GET YOU SOMETHING TOMORROW, JUGGIE, THAT'LL KEEP THOSE SCREAMING FEMALES AT BAY!
YOU WILL?

NEXT DAY-
YOU BOUGHT A WHOLE NEW SET OF DRUMS FOR THAT CREEP?
THEY MUST'VE COST YOU A FORTUNE!
IT'S ONLY MONEY!

AND HIS DRUMMING DROWNS OUT HIS SINGING, WHICH THE FANS FIND SO REVOLTINGLY SEXY!
GOOD THINKING! NOW MAYBE THEY'LL APPRECIATE THE REAL STARS OF THIS GROUP- YOU AND ME!
IS HE SINGING?
WHO KNOWS?
BAM!
The Archies
RAT TAT TAT TAT
BOOM BOOM!
5
END

The Archies in "REGGIE MANTLE, SUPER STAR"
HEY, FELLOWS! HERE'S OUR CHANCE TO BREAK INTO THE MOVIES!
HUH ? WHY DO YOU WANT TO SNEAK INTO THE MOVIES ? DON'T YOU HAVE ANY MONEY ?
I'M NOT TALKING ABOUT THE THEATRE, DUMMY! MISTER STARFINDER IS IN TOWN!
WHO IS MISTER STARFINDER ?
HE'S A MOVIE TALENT SCOUT AND HE'S HERE IN RIVERDALE!
1

THEY SAY HE'S LOOKING FOR SOME KIDS TO PLAY PARTS IN A NEW MOVIE ABOUT THE YOUTH OF TODAY! THEY'RE GIVING SCREEN TESTS DOWN AT THE T.V. STUDIO!
THAT'S GREAT, REGGIE! WE'LL GO DOWN AND SEE IF WE CAN GET AN AUDITION!
The Archies
ARE YOU FLAKY, MAN ? ALL THE TEEN-AGE YOUTH OF RIVERDALE WILL BE AT THAT T.V. STUDIO!
WE HAVE TO BEAT THEM ALL TO THE PUNCH, AND I KNOW JUST HOW WE'RE GOING TO DO IT!
?
ALL THE BIG SHOTS WHO COME IN THIS TOWN STAY AT THE RIVERDALE TILTON, AND THAT'S JUST WHERE WE'RE GOING! COME ON!
BUT HOW CAN YOU BE SURE HE'LL BE THERE ?
2

BECAUSE I'M CERTAIN, ARCH.!
AND WHAT IF HE DOESN'T WANT TO BE DISTURBED AT THE HOTEL?
the Archies

YOU JUST LEAVE IT TO REGGIE, FELLOWS.! I'LL FIGURE SOMETHING OUT.!
RDALE
TON
PARKI

WILL YOU KINDLY TELL MISTER STARFINDER THAT REGGIE MANTLE, SUPER STAR OF THE ARCHIES, IS HERE TO SEE HIM?
I'M SORRY, BUT WE DON'T HAVE ANY MISTER STARFINDER REGISTERED HERE.!

YOU CAN LEVEL WITH ME, MAC! YOU SEE, HE TOLD ME PERSONALLY HE WAS STAYING HERE.!

YOU MUST BE MISTAKEN, YOUNG MAN.! THERE'S NO SUCH PERSON IN THIS HOTEL.!
OKAY.! HAVE IT YOUR WAY.!
3

WELL, I GUESS HE'S NOT STAYING HERE, REG.!
ARE YOU FOR REAL, ARCH.? THEY ALWAYS SAY THAT WHEN THEY HAVE SOMEBODY LIKE MISTER STARFINDER IN THEIR HOTEL.! IT'S FOR HIS PROTECTION, OTHERWISE HE'D BE PESTERED BY A BUNCH OF TEENAGE KIDS.!
RT
RIVERDALE TILT

I TOOK A QUICK GLANCE AT THE REGISTER! I THINK HE'S IN ROOM 61!
BUT HE WON'T LET US UPSTAIRS.!
LTON

COME ON.! WE'RE GOING TO SNEAK IN THE BACK WAY, THROUGH THE HOTEL KITCHEN.!
?

DO YOU THINK WE SHOULD, REGGIE? WHY DON'T WE JUST TAKE OUR CHANCES AT THE T.V. STUDIO.?
DON'T BE SILLY, ARCH.! THIS WAY WE'LL GET A PERSONAL AUDITION.! NOW JUST FOLLOW ME.! I KNOW WHAT I'M DOING.!
KITCHEN DELIVERY ENTRANCE
4

NOW BE QUIET!

?

HEY! JUST WHAT DO YOU THINK YOU'RE DOING?
?
5

PUT THAT FOOD BACK AND COME OVER HERE.! YOU DON'T BELONG IN HERE! WHAT ARE YOU KIDS UP TO?
GULP!
OH, NO! THAT BEAN BAG!

COME ON! LET'S GET MOVING!
STOP, YOU KIDS!

WHAT'S GOING ON? WHAT'S ALL THE SHOUTING ABOUT?
THERE WERE A COUPLE OF KIDS IN MY KITCHEN STEALING FOOD! THEY'RE AROUND HERE SOMEWHERE!
6

WHAT ARE YOU TRYING TO DO, JUG, GET US ALL IN TROUBLE? IS THAT ALL YOU EVER THINK OF... FOOD?
I COULDN'T HELP MYSELF! IT SMELLED SO GOOD, I JUST WANTED TO SAMPLE IT!

NOW THEY'LL BE LOOKING FOR US ALL OVER THE HOTEL! YOU MEATHEAD!
WHY DON'T WE JUST FORGET THIS WHOLE IDEA? IT'S FLAKY!

WHAT? AND GIVE UP A CHANCE TO GET INTO SHOW BIZ? NEVER!
OPPORTUNITY COULD BE WAITING FOR US RIGHT AROUND THE CORNER!
AND THAT'S NOT ALL!
39
47-70
7

HERE'S ROOM 61.! NOW LET'S BELT OUT A TUNE THAT WILL MAKE HIM JUMP UP AND TAKE NOTICE.!

OKAY, BUT I HOPE HE DOESN'T BELT US BACK.!

60

61

BAM A DE BAM!

WHAT THE HECK IS GOING ON OUT HERE ?

DO YOU LIKE IT, MISTER STARFINDER ?

LIKE IT ?

8

LET'S SEE HOW YOU LIKE THIS.!
?
BOP!

AND THE NAME IS NOT STAR-FINDER.! SO GET OUT OF HERE AND LET ME GET SOME SLEEP.!
61
SLAM!
63

I KNOW WHAT I DID WRONG, FELLOWS.!
SO DO I.! YOU GOT UP THIS MORNING.!
I'LL BET I LOOKED AT THAT ROOM REGISTER UPSIDE DOWN.! IT WASN'T ROOM 61, IT'S ROOM 19.!
?
9

FORGET IT, REG.! I COULDN'T TAKE ANY-MORE AUDITIONS LIKE THAT!

COME ON, ARCH.! NOTHING'S GOING TO MAKE ME QUIT! I'M DETERMINED TO BE DISCOVERED!

WELL, ARE YOU CONVINCED THAT WAS A LOUSY IDEA?

NO! IT WAS JUST OUR BAD LUCK WE DIDN'T GO TO ROOM 19 FIRST! NOW IF I COULD FIGURE OUT ANOTHER WAY!
?

FORGET IT, REG! YOU CAN COUNT US OUT!
THAT'S WHAT'S WRONG WITH YOU GUYS! YOU HAVE NO DRIVE, NO PERSEVERANCE. BUT TAKE ME, I'M DETERMINED TO BE A STAR!
PA

THEN WE SHOULD HAVE GONE OVER TO THE T.V. STUDIO AND TRIED OUR LUCK! NOW IT'S PROBABLY TOO LATE!

WITH A MOB LIKE THEY WOULD HAVE HAD OVER THERE WE WOULDN'T EVEN BE NOTICED!
The Archies

SO THERE YOU ARE, ARCHIE! I'VE BEEN LOOKING ALL OVER FOR YOU FELLOWS!

THERE WAS A MISTER STAR-FINDER AT THE HOUSE! HE WANTED TO TALK TO THE ARCHIES!
!?

IT WAS SOMETHING ABOUT AN AUDITION FOR A MOVIE, BUT HE COULDN'T WAIT ANY LONGER! HE HAD TO FLY BACK TO THE COAST!
GULP!

WHAT ARE YOU FELLOWS DOING?
WE'RE GOING TO USE OUR DRIVE AND PERSEVERANCE AND MAKE REGGIE A SUPER STAR!
OR A TRACK ONE!
END

THE Archies in SIGN OFF!

VERY CLASSY ACT, GUYS! WHAT DO YOU DO FOR AN ENCORE?

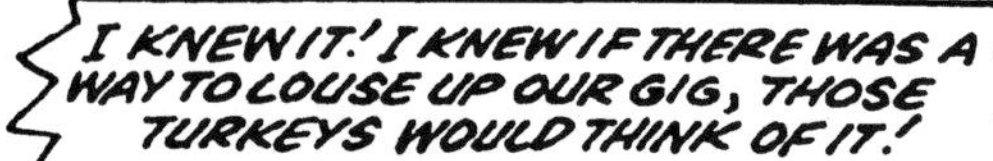
I KNEW IT! I KNEW IF THERE WAS A WAY TO LOUSE UP OUR GIG, THOSE TURKEYS WOULD THINK OF IT!

AS OBNOXIOUS AS NEEDLE-NOSE IS, WE STILL NEED HIS BEAT!

RONNIE'S RIGHT! HOW ARE WE GOING TO PLAY A GIG WITHOUT A DRUM?

IF YOU TWO WOULD JUST GROW UP, MAYBE WE COULD MAKE A SUCCESS OUT OF THIS GROUP!

OKAY! OKAY! OKAY! ENOUGH, ALREADY!! STOP WITH THE NAGGING!!

WE'LL TAKE THIS THING AND WE'LL EITHER GET IT REPAIRED OR REPLACED!
BY EIGHT O'CLOCK TONIGHT, AND DON'T FORGET IT!
2

-AND ONE LAST WORD, BEFORE YOU LEAVE--
DON'T TRY TO KID US! WE WEREN'T BORN YESTERDAY!
AR

WITH YOU TWO, THERE'S NO SUCH THING AS A "LAST" WORD!!
ROAR

SHEESH! YOU'D THINK WE STARTED WORLD WAR THREE!!

ONE LITTLE MISTAKE AND THOSE TWO PULL THE PLUG ON YOU!
MAN! YOU'D THINK WE NEVER DID ANYTHING RIGHT!
YEAH!
The ARCHIES

TAKE IT TO BOOM BOOM BARRY! THAT'S WHERE JUGHEAD GETS ALL HIS DRUM WORK DONE!
RIGHT!

WE DID KINDA WRECK IT, DIDN'T WE?
IT WAS JUGHEAD'S FAULT! HE RUINED A MIGHTY FINE PASS!
BOOM BOOM BARRY
DRUMS
3

MY! MY! I THINK THAT DRUMHEAD HAS LOST A BIT OF TENSION!
MAYBE THE MOTHS GOT AT IT!

HEY! WE HAVE A GIG TONIGHT! THIS THING'S GOTTA BE REPAIRED OR RE-PLACED IN A HURRY!
WE'LL HAVE TO GET YOU ONE, I GUESS!

HOW ABOUT THIS? IT'S ABOUT THE SAME MODEL!
GREAT!

ER- JUST ONE THING!
YEAH?

WE GOTTA HAVE THE NAME OF OUR GROUP ON THE DRUMHEAD!

IT'S GONNA COST YOU EXTRA 'CAUSE WE'LL HAVE TO REMOVE THE NAME WHEN YOU RETURN THE DRUM!
FORGET IT! THE NAME'S NOT IMPORTANT!

THE HECK IT'S NOT!
HERE! WRITE OUT WHAT YOU WANT AND WE'LL HAVE IT FOR YOU BY TONIGHT!
4

THEIR DRUMMER SURE HAS A HEAVY HAND WITH THE STICKS!
THAT REDHEAD IS GONNA BE A DOCTOR, I BETCHA!

WHAT MAKES YOU SAY THAT?
'CAUSE HE'LL BE ABLE TO WRITE PRESCRIPTIONS NOBODY CAN UNDER-STAND!

LOOK AT THOSE HENTRACKS, WILL YOU? THERE! THIS IS ABOUT AS CLOSE AS I CAN COME! WHAT DO YOU THINK?
?

WITH THE CRAZY NAMES THEY USE THESE DAYS...THAT MUST BE IT! IT'S THE ONLY WORD I CAN MAKE OUT OF THAT SCRAWL!

WHEN NEW METHODS OF HUMILIATION ARE INVENTED - THOSE TWO WILL BE RESPONSIBLE!
THANKS A HEAP, ARCH!
"THE ANCHOVIES"? NOW THAT'S A FISHY OUTFIT!
YOU REALLY GOT TO WORK ON YOUR HANDWRITING, PAL!
The ANCHOVIES
END.

THE Archies in "FED UP WITH ARCHIE"

LOOK AT THE BRIGHT SIDE, VERONICA! WHAT ELSE COULD HE POSSIBLY DO WRONG?
THANKS, BETTY! I THINK?!

SPUTTER! SPUTTER!
I JUST HAD TO SAY THAT, DIDN'T I?!
HMMM! IT DIED! WHAT COULD'VE CAUSED THAT?!

THE FACT THAT THE GAS NEEDLE IS ON "E" COULD BE A CLUE!
OH?!

LET ME AT HIM! LET ME AT HIM! NO COURT WILL EVER CONVICT ME!
WHOA! EASY, GIRL! HE'S GOT TO BE IN SHAPE TO GET MORE GAS!

SOON...
JUG, WILL YOU GO WITH ME TO FIND A GAS STATION?
I'M AFRAID MY HUNGER'S TOO ADVANCED! I'D ONLY SLOW YOU DOWN! BUT IF YOU HAPPEN TO SEE A FOOD PLACE...

THAT'S IT! I'LL TAKE FOOD ORDERS! MAYBE THERE'LL BE A RESTAURANT NEARBY, TOO!
THAT'S THE BRIGHTEST IDEA YOU'VE HAD ALL NIGHT!
2

REMEMBER, NO TOMATOES ON MY BURGER AND HOLD THE KETCHUP!
ADD SIX MORE ORDERS OF ONION RINGS TO MY ORDER!
AND I PREFER MY BURGER MEDIUM RARE!
SCRATCH! SCRATCH!

GOT IT! I'LL GRAB THE GAS CAN AND I'M OUTTA HERE!
THAT'S NICE!
TRUE LOVE

DOWN THE ROAD...
A BURGER TIME! THERE MUST BE A GAS STATION NEARBY!
BURGER TIME
GAS

BACK AT THE VAN...
HEY! WHAT'S THAT PIECE OF PAPER ON ARCHIE'S SEAT?!
OUR ORDERS!! OUR FEARLESS LEADER'S STAYING TRUE TO FORM!
SIGH ARE ANY PARTS OF A MINI-VAN EDIBLE?!

LATER...
AND SO, AS THE STORY GOES, THE OLD MAN WITH THE HOOK STILL WANDERS DOWN THE HIGHWAY LOOKING FOR HIS NEXT VICTIMS!
CHATTER! CHATTER!

TAP! TAP! TAP!
AAARGH!
3

TELLING THE " OLD MAN WITH THE HOOK" STORY AGAIN, HUH, REGGIE?
HMMPH!
FOOD!
I HOPE THIS ISN'T ANOTHER HALLUCINATION!
ARCHIE, IT PAINS ME, BUT I'VE GOT TO APOLOGIZE! THIS FOOD IS GREAT!
AND IT'S AMAZING HOW YOU GOT ALL OUR ORDERS RIGHT WITHOUT THAT LIST!
CHOMP CHOMP
CHOMP
WHAT CAN I SAY? I'VE GOT A MIND LIKE A STEEL TRAP!
YOU EVEN GOT THEM TO HOLD MY ONIONS, YOU LITTLE DICKENS!
WELL, MR. STEEL TRAP, ONCE YOU GET THROUGH EATING, PUT THAT GAS IN AND WE'LL BE ON OUR WAY!
GAS?!
GAS
DARN! I JUST KNEW THERE WAS SOMETHING ELSE!
END

THE Archies "NAME OF THE GAME"

YOU WANT TO HAVE A *WHAT?*

A P.R. MAN! PUBLIC RELATIONS! HE'LL PUT US ON THE MAP!

THAT'S A FANTASTIC IDEA!

WHO WANTS TO BE ON THE MAP? WE'RE A MUSICAL GROUP, NOT A MAJOR HIGHWAY!

EVERYBODY CAN USE PUBLICITY!

"THE ARCHIES" ARE A HOUSEHOLD WORD!

SO IS "*DIRT*"!

I SAY WE GIVE IT A TRY!

WHERE ARE WE GOING TO FIND A PUBLIC RELATIONS MAN?

I THOUGHT YOU'D NEVER ASK!

FINEST DECISION YOU EVER MADE, FOLKS! IN NO TIME AT ALL YOUR NAME WILL BE ON EVERYBODY'S LIPS!

-BY THE WAY- WHAT IS THE NAME?

"THE ARCHIES"!
NO WONDER NO ONE KNOWS YOU!

FIRST THING WE DO IS GET RID OF THE NAME! THAT'S GOT TO GO!
2

NO WAY! WHAT'S WRONG WITH THE NAME?
LET ME COUNT THE WAYS!

IT'S ALWAYS BEEN A SAPPY NAME!
IT'S BETTER THAN "THE REGGIES"!

I SAY WE LET OUR P.R. MAN HANDLE IT!

HOW ABOUT "BLUE SUGAR"-"DRIVE-TRAIN"-"DEEP SIXES"-"COFFIN NAILS"?
MARVELOUS! I LIKE THEM ALL!

THE PROBLEM IS IN PICKING OUT THE BEST NAME!
I STILL LIKE "THE ARCHIES"!

WHY DON'T WE RUN A TEST?
WHAT KIND OF TEST?

I'LL GET POSTERS MADE USING EACH OF THE FOUR NAMES!
AND?
3

WE SET THEM UP OUT-SIDE WHERE YOU'RE PLAYING - LIKE YOU'RE FOUR DIFFERENT GROUPS!

THEN WE SEE WHICH ONE DRAWS MORE ATTENTION!

THE MAN'S A GENIUS!
IT'S YOUR BALL, PAL - RUN WITH IT!

WE HAVE TO PAY THIS GUY TO THINK UP SILLY NAMES FOR US?
WE OUGHTA CALL OURSELVES "SUCKERS FIVE"!

HEY, WE COULDN'T HAVE HAD A SILLIER NAME THAN "THE ARCHIES"!

THAT NITE:
I'LL SET THESE UP AND WATCH THE REACTIONS OUT HERE!
TONITE

MEANWHILE, WE HAVE TO GO TO WORK! LET'S GO!
TONITE
BLUE SUGAR
TONITE
DRIVETRAIN
DEEP SIX
4

LATER -
WHAT'S GOING ON? WE'VE BEEN PLAYING FOR AN HOUR AND NOBODY'S COME IN!

MAYBE WE'RE LOSING OUR TOUCH!
IT SURE HAPPENED FAST!

WHERE IS EVERY-BODY? LAST NIGHT THE PLACE WAS JUMPING!
ANAGER

I'D BETTER CHECK THE DOOR! MAYBE SOME-BODY FORGOT TO UNLOCK IT!

NO, IT'S NOT THAT! THE DOOR IS OPEN!

WHAT THE HECK ARE THESE THINGS?
UE
AR
TONITE
DRIVETRA

I DON'T HAVE ANY OF THESE GROUPS PLAYING IN MY PLACE!
UE
AR
TONITE
DRIVETRAIN
THE DEEP SIX
5

WHO'S THE CREEP WHO'S SABOTAGING MY BUSINESS?
WHAT DO YOU MEAN?

SOMEBODY PUT A BUNCH OF DUMB POSTERS OUTSIDE!
THEY'RE SUPPOSED TO DRAW CUSTOMERS INTO YOUR ESTABLISH-MENT!

WELL, IT'S DRIVING THEM AWAY! THEY TAKE ONE LOOK AND THEY GO ELSEWHERE!

THE ONLY GROUP THEY WANT TO SEE IN HERE IS *THE ARCHIES*!

WELL, SO MUCH FOR PUBLIC RELATIONS!
WELCOME BACK, ARCHIES!!
HOW ABOUT "RIGOR MORTIS"? "ZOMBIEVILLE"? "THE FLATWHEEL FIVE"?
The END

THE Archies in "ROCK N' ROLL IS HERE TO ~~STAY~~ SEE"

ON THE OTHER HAND, SOME OF THOSE ROCK ACTS ON TV CAN BE VERY BORING!
TRANSLATED, THAT MEANS REGGIE ISN'T PART OF THEM!
CHIP COOKIES

IT'S 2:15!
AND IN ANOTHER MINUTE IT'LL BE 2:16!

COME ALONG! WE DON'T HAVE A MINUTE TO LOSE!
?

I CHECKED WITH THE NTV PROGRAMMING BEFORE!
AND?
RIVERDALE SHOPPING CENTER

AND THEY'RE ABOUT TO PREVIEW OUR NEW TAPE! WE'RE IN FOR A SUPER TREAT!
AL'S APPLIANCES
?

PRESENTING THE ARCHIES!
HERE WE CAN WATCH OURSELVES SIMULTANEOUSLY ON OVER THIRTY SCREENS!
I DON'T BELIEVE THIS!
SALE $495
2

HATED TO PULL YOU AWAY FROM ALL THOSE TV SCREENS, REG, BUT WE HAVE A REHEARSAL SESSION COMING UP!
WE HAVE TO TAKE CARE OF BUSINESS FIRST!
I'M ONE STEP AHEAD OF YOU!

I HAVE SOMEONE COMING OVER WHO'S GOING TO MAKE OUR GROUP #1!
NO KIDDING!
REHEARSAL STUDIO 1 FLIGHT UP

IS IT A NEW PRODUCER, OR A HOTSHOT SONG-WRITER?
OH, IT'S SOME-ONE BIGGER THAN THAT!

BECAUSE THE VISUAL IS SO IMPORTANT, NOWADAYS A GROUP NEEDS A GREAT HAIRSTYLIST TO MAKE IT ON ROCK VIDEO!
CALL ME 'ZIGGY'!

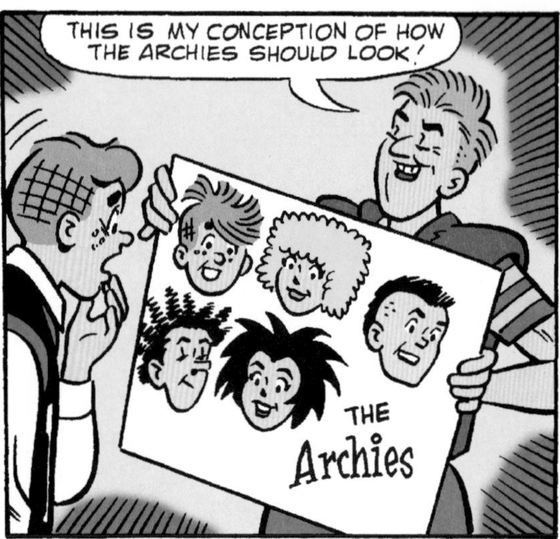
THIS IS MY CONCEPTION OF HOW THE ARCHIES SHOULD LOOK!
THE Archies

SORRY, ZIGGY! BUT WE'RE HAPPY WITH OUR PRESENT IMAGE!
HMPF! YOU'RE PROBABLY THE ONLY ONES WHO ARE!
STUDIO B
3

REG, SOME OF US DON'T WANT TO CHANGE OUR APPEARANCE!
IT'S OKAY! I FIGURED OUT A WAY AROUND THAT PROBLEM, TOO!

SINCE YOU'RE SO HOMELY-LOOKING WE COULD GET A STAND-IN FOR YOU WHEN WE TAPE A ROCK VIDEO!

DO ME A FAVOR, REG! LET'S FORGET ABOUT ROCK VIDEOS FOR A WHILE!

IN THE MEANTIME, YOU CAN GO GET OUR VAN READY FOR TONIGHT'S GIG!
GOTCHA, EXALTED LEADER!

ONE HOUR LATER...
WHAT'S TAKING REGGIE SO LONG?
I'M GETTING THE VAN READY LIKE YOU TOLD ME!
THE Archies

I'M INSTALLING A VIDEO MACHINE SO WE CAN WATCH OUR TAPES EN ROUTE TO OUR GIGS!
4

HEY! WE'VE REALLY TURNED ON OUR CROWD!
IT'S A PLEASURE TO BE PLAYING AND NOT HAVE TO LISTEN TO REG CARRY ON ABOUT ROCK VIDEOS!
THE Archies

THIS IS A REAL CLASSY PLACE, REG!
I HAVE TO ADMIT YOU DID WELL IN BOOKING US HERE!

THIS PLACE IS BETTER THAN YOU GUYS THINK!
HAVE YOU SEEN THEIR LOUNGE?

THEY HAVE ONE OF THOSE NEW GIANT SCREENS!
NOW WE'LL BE ABLE TO WATCH OURSELVES EVEN DURING OUR BREAKS!
The End

THE Archies in "GROUP WHOOP"

D-UH, WE WORK AS HARD AS ANY-ONE IN "THE ARCHIES"!
WHY SHOULDN'T WE HAVE A SAY ABOUT THE DIRECTION THE GROUP TAKES?
'CAUSE EVERYONE KNOWS ROADIES JUST HANDLE EQUIPMENT!
ONLY THE MUSICIANS GET INVOLVED IN THE CREATIVE AREA!

DILT, WHAT DO I DO WITH THIS STUFF YOU WANTED TO SHOW "THE ARCHIES"!?
OH, JUST PUT IT IN THE VAN!
--- I STILL THINK MY IDEA WAS A GOOD ONE!

HOURS LATER --
HOW ABOUT PLAYING MIDDLE-OF-THE-ROAD-ROCK?
SPEAKING OF ROADS-

---WE'D BETTER HIT THE ROAD, OR WE WON'T GET TO OUR CONCERT IN TIME!
2

THE EQUIPMENT IS ALL SET UP, DILTON!
GOOD WORK, MOOSE!
The Archies

WHERE ARE "THE ARCHIES"? THEY'RE SCHEDULED TO GO ON IN ONLY HALF AN HOUR!
NO SWEAT, MR. ROGERS, THEY'LL BE HERE IN TIME!

I KNEW WE SHOULD HAVE LEFT SOONER!
HOW WERE WE SUPPOSED TO KNOW WE'D HIT A BIG TRAFFIC JAM?

I MAY NOT KNOW WHAT'LL PLEASE TONIGHT'S AUDIENCE---
BUT I DO KNOW WHAT'LL DISPLEASE 'EM -- OUR SHOWING UP LATE!
4 SALE
3

YOUR GROUP IS ALREADY TEN MINUTES LATE!
SOMETHING MUST HAVE HELD THEM UP!

HMM! IS IT OKAY IF MOOSE AND I ENTERTAIN THE AUDIENCE 'TIL "THE ARCHIES" GET HERE?
SURE! SURE! ANYTHING IS BETTER THAN NO ACT AT ALL!

WOW! WE'RE ALREADY A HALF-HOUR LATE!
I'LL BET THE AUDIENCE IS IN A RAGE!
SOUTHVILLE
AUDIT

LISTEN! SOMEBODY IS ALREADY PLAYING!

WELL, I'LL BE!
IT'S MOOSE AND DILTON--- PLAYING COUNTRY AND WESTERN!

"COUNTRY AND WESTERN"? THAT'S RIDICULOUS!
WHAT'S "RIDICULOUS"? THE CROWD IS DIGGING IT!
4

LISTEN TO THE OVATION THEY'RE GETTING!
I GUESS THAT SETTLES THE KIND OF MUSIC WE'LL BE PLAYING TONIGHT!

BUT, ARCHIE, WE'RE NOT DRESSED FOR COUNTRY AND WESTERN!

D-UH, THAT'S WHAT DILTON WAS TRYING TO SHOW YOU!
MOOSE AND I HAD ALREADY OBTAINED WESTERN GEAR FOR "THE ARCHIES"!

DILTON, THIS PROVES YOU AND I ARE THE BEST ROADIES IN THE BUSINESS!
HOW SO?

WE KNOW WHAT "THE ARCHIES" WILL NEED EVEN BEFORE THEY DO!
The Archies
END

The Archies in "Bubble Trouble"

IS VANCE FORWARD REALLY GOOD?
BETTY, VANCE IS NUMERO UNO WHEN IT COMES TO PRODUCING ROCK VIDEOS!
FORWARD PRODUCTIONS
ARCHIES

HI, VANCE! WE'RE ALL SET!
SORRY, GUYS! WE'VE DECIDED TO CANCEL YOUR VIDEO!

WE NEED A CONCEPT FOR YOU, AND I CAN'T THINK OF ONE!

YOU JUST DON'T HAVE AN IMAGE! IT'D BE DIFFERENT IF YOU GUYS WERE INTO HEAVY METAL...

...OR IF YOU WERE ONE OF THE NEW WAVE BANDS!
FORWARD PRODUCTION PRESENTS

BY ANY CHANCE, DID McNASTY'S COLUMN HAVE SOMETHING TO DO WITH YOUR DECISION?
YEAH, AS A MATTER OF FACT, IT DID!
2

ARCHIE, I DON'T SEE HOW IT'LL HELP US TO CONFRONT McNASTY!
IT'S WORTH A TRY!
GROANING STONE MAGAZINE

MR. McNASTY, WE'RE THE...
YEAH, I KNOW! YOU'RE THE ARCHIES!

I'M SORRY, KIDS, BUT I HAVE TO BE HONEST!
...YOUR SOUND IS PURE UNADULTERATED BUBBLEGUM!

DON'T LISTEN TO HIM, ARCHIE!
CRITICS ARE ALWAYS PUTTING DOWN OTHER PEOPLE TO MAKE THEMSELVES IMPORTANT!

MAYBE HE'S RIGHT! MAYBE THE ARCHIES ARE NOTHING BUT...

JUGHEAD! YOU'VE JUST GIVEN ME THE CONCEPT!
GULP! IS IT CONTAGIOUS?
3

WE'RE GOING BACK TO SEE MR. VANCE!

BEFORE WE GET THERE I WANT YOU ALL TO HELP YOURSELVES TO SOME OF THIS! NOW HERE'S MY PLAN...
BUBBLE GUM

MR. VANCE, I THINK WE HAVE THE CONCEPT THAT WAS ELUDING YOU!
YOU HAVE?

THE ARCHIES ARE THE LEADERS OF GOOD-TIME BUBBLEGUM ROCK AND PROUD OF IT!
HMM!

YOU'RE RIGHT! I CAN SEE IT NOW!
...THE ARCHIES APPEAR IN A GREAT BIG PINK BUBBLE!...SURROUNDED BY HUNDREDS OF FANS ALL CHEWING BUBBLE-GUM!

JIMMY, GET THOSE CAMERAS ROLLING!
...WE'RE GONNA SHOOT THE ARCHIES, BY GUM!
STUDI
B
4

WOW! THIS IS GOING TO BE MY BEST VIDEO YET!

LATER:
FOR THE THIRD WEEK IN A ROW THE ARCHIES' BUBBLEGUM VIDEO IS #1!
YAHOO!

RAP McNASTY IS HERE TO INTERVIEW US!
McNASTY IS GOING TO HAVE TO APOLOGIZE TO THE ARCHIES FIRST!

GANG, I THINK HE ALREADY HAS!
END

THE Archies in "THE SHRINE"

MAYBE SOMEDAY THERE'LL BE A SHRINE DEDICATED TO THE ARCHIES!

DREAM ON!

HA! THE ULTIMATE FANTASY!

PARKING LOT 2

GUESTS ARE REQUESTED TO SPEAK IN WHISPERS WHILE VISITING THE HALLOWED MUSEUM GROUND DEDICATED TO THE ARCHIES!

THIS IS THE ACTUAL GARAGE WHERE THE ARCHIES FIRST REHEARSED! IT WAS MOVED HERE BRICK BY BRICK!

PLEASE, SIR! DON'T STEP ON THAT GREASE SPOT!
...IT WAS MADE BY A VAN BELONGING TO THE ARCHIES AND IS IRREPLACE-ABLE!

THIS GUITAR ACTUALLY BELONGED TO ARCHIE!
...YOU MAY RUB IT FOR ONE DOLLAR!

MA'AM! I SAW YOU SNEAK IN AN EXTRA RUB!
...THAT'LL BE TWO DOLLARS!
2

AND HERE'S THE *UNIQUE HAT* THAT BELONGED TO DRUMMER JUGHEAD JONES!
...THERE'S NOT ANOTHER HAT QUITE LIKE IT IN THE *WHOLE WORLD*!
JUGHEAD'S HAT
TOUR GUIDE

...EXCEPT FOR A FEW THOUSAND THAT WE STILL HAVE IN OUR SOUVENIR SHOP!
JUGHEAD HATS $12.95

FANS OF THE ARCHIES HAVE ALWAYS WANTED AN INSIDE LOOK INTO THAT FABULOUS GROUP!
THE ARCHIES

...SO HERE'S AN INSIDE LOOK INTO JUGHEAD'S DRUM!
TOUR GUIDE
CHIPS
COOKIES
PEANUT BUTTER

REGGIE MANTLE WAS ALWAYS TRYING TO STEAL THE SPOTLIGHT FROM THE REST OF THE GROUP!
COSTUME BELONGING TO REGGIE MANTLE

AND AT ONE PERFORMANCE HE ACTUALLY *DID* STEAL THE SPOTLIGHT!
...REGGIE BRIBED A LIGHTING TECHNICIAN TO TRAIN THIS SPOT-LIGHT ON HIMSELF!
3

IT IS DEFINITELY NOT TRUE THAT BETTY AND VERONICA FOUGHT OVER ARCHIE EVERY NIGHT!
STAGE WIGS BELONGING TO BETTY AND VERONICA
YOUR GUIDE

...IT WAS MORE LIKE EVERY OTHER NIGHT!

LADIES AND GENTLEMEN! THE GREAT ARCHIE ANDREWS HAS JUST ARRIVED IN PERSON!

PLEASE, FOLKS! DON'T RUSH ME!
...I'M FALLING !!!

KRASH!

YOU FELL OFF YOUR SEAT, ARCHIE!
GEE! THE DREAM SEEMED SO REAL!
COLA
4

GOSH! WHAT A DREAM I JUST HAD!
...THE ARCHIES WERE RICH AND FAMOUS BEYOND OUR WILDEST FANTASIES!
THE
RCHIES

HA! THAT'S A LAUGH AND A HALF!
MOST PEOPLE DON'T KNOW US FROM A HOLE IN A DOUGHNUT!

CAN WE HAVE YOUR AUTOGRAPH PLEASE?
SURE, GIRLS!

THOSE FANS JUST ASKED ME FOR MY AUTOGRAPH!
...THAT PROVES WE ARE FAMOUS!

WE DID IT, LUCEY! WE DID IT!
YEAH - WE GOT THE LAST ITEM ON OUR SCAVENGER HUNT LIST!

THE AUTOGRAPH OF AN UNKNOWN ROCK GROUP LEADER!
END